CHOOSE YOUR OWN ADVENTURE®

Fans Love Reading
Choose Your Own Adventure®!

"Come on in this book if you're crazy enough!
One wrong move and you're a goner!"
Ben Curley, Age 9

"I like this book because it's like you're
writing your own book!"
Kyle Smart, Age 5

"Sometimes I'm scared because I
don't know what will happen. Then I just
make a different choice."
Natasha Burbank, Age 9

"If you want to go on a magnificent adventure
of your choice, go to page 1 and begin reading.
If you don't then get another book!"
Quillyn Peterson, Age 9

Lost Dog! ©1985 R.A. Montgomery
Warren, Vermont. All Rights Reserved.

Artwork, design, and revised text ©2011 Chooseco, LLC,
Waitsfield, Vermont. All Rights Reserved.

Illustrated by Keith Newton
Book and cover design by Julia Gignoux, Stacey Boyd
For information regarding permission, write to:

CHOOSECO

P.O. Box 46
Waitsfield, Vermont 05673
www.cyoa.com

A DRAGONLARK BOOK

ISBN: 1-933390-00-X
EAN: 978-1-933390-00-0

Published simultaneously in the United States and Canada

Printed in China.

12 11 10 9 8 7 6 5 4

R OWN ADVENTURE®

LOST DOG!

BY R. A. MONTGOMERY

ILLUSTRATED BY KEITH NEWTON

A DRAGONLARK BOOK

Where's your dog Homer?

He's not on the porch. He's not behind the garage, either.

"Homer! Hey, Homer!" you call. "Where are you?"

There is no answering bark. Homer had to spend last night outside because he'd chewed up a shoe. (This time it was Dad's shoe.) He must have wandered away!

You run into the living room.

"Dad! Dad! Homer's lost. He's run away!" you shout.

Turn to the next page.

Your dad lowers the paper he is reading and looks over the top of his glasses.

"You always get too excited," he says. "Homer is *not* lost. He'll come home."

The paper goes back up.

Go on to the next page.

Next you try your mother.

"Mom, Homer's gone!"

Your mom is too busy to help.

You try your older brother.

"Beat it, squirt," he says. "I've got important things to do. No time for dogs or little kids. Beat it!"

Turn to the next page.

Just then your younger sister, Jessica, comes up to you.

"I'll help," she says. "We could go to the radio station. They report lost dogs and cats."

Go on to the next page.

"Good old Jessica. It's nice to have *some-one* I can count on!" you say.

But maybe you should look down by the fort in the woods first. It's one of Homer's favorite places.

If you go to the local radio station in town, turn to page 7.

If you decide to look down by the fort in the woods, turn to page 10.

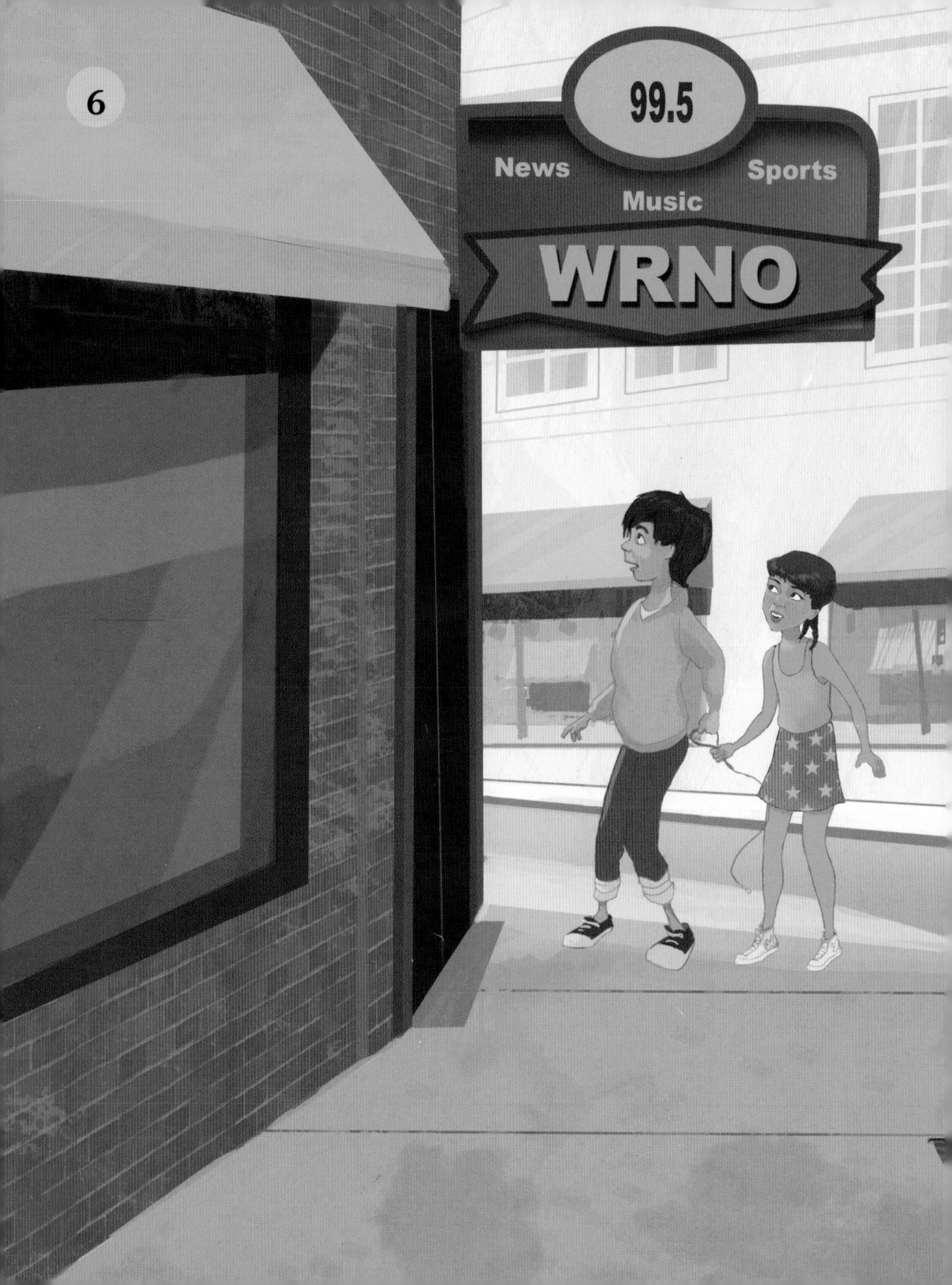
99.5
News
Sports
Music
WRNO

"I'm not sure this is going to work," you tell Jessica. "Homer doesn't listen to the radio, you know."

"I'm not stupid!" Jessica answers. "People will hear 'Pet Parade' and report Homer if they see him."

The radio station is in a small brick building near your house. You get there in about ten minutes.

Turn to page 9.

"Who's going to do the talking?" you ask. "It was your idea, Jessica."

"Yeah, but Homer is your dog," she replies.

If you insist that Jessica do the talking, turn to page 18.

If you decide to do the talking, turn to page 24.

"Homer loves the fort, Jessica. Follow me," you say.

"I don't know. Those older kids who built it are *mean!*" says Jessica.

"I know, but we've got to find Homer," you reply.

Soon you come to a clearing in the woods. The fort is built on a platform way up in the biggest tree. You and Jessica stand behind another tree.

"Quiet, Jessica," you say.

"Why?" she whispers.

Turn to page 12.

"Schooner the bully is there!"

Schooner is talking loudly to two other boys.

"We'll be rich! Rich, I tell you! Hey, what's that noise? Is there anyone out there?"

Schooner stares right at the spot where you're hiding!

If you stay where you are and keep quiet, go on to the next page.

If you run for it, turn to page 14.

"Don't move, Jessica," you whisper. "He doesn't really see us."

"Okay," she whispers back.

Schooner turns away and goes on talking to the others. You catch a few more of his words. He's talking about Old Pete!

Old Pete lives all alone in a little cabin. He's very smart, and he's a good friend of your dad's.

"We'll break into the old guy's house. He hides his money in a big tin can under the floorboards. I've seen him," says Schooner.

Turn to page 17.

"Run for it, Jessica!" you yell.

Schooner grabs a big stick. He charges after you and Jessica!

"If Homer were here...oh, I wish Homer were here! He'd save us," Jessica says.

"Yeah," you reply. "Old Homer would take care of Schooner."

Just at that very moment Homer appears out of nowhere!

"Homer! Homer, where were you?" you shout.

But Schooner is almost on top of you.

If you decide to stay and face Schooner with Homer's help, turn to page 35.

If you keep on running, turn to page 38.

"But he's got a dog. I saw it this morning. A big brown-and-black dog," says one of the boys.

"No! That's not his dog. That's just some mutt who comes by looking for handouts now and then. No trouble with him if he's still there."

You turn to Jessica. "It must be Homer! Homer likes Old Pete. He visits him a lot."

"What do we do now?" Jessica asks.

If you decide to go home for help, turn to page 46.

If you decide to run to Old Pete's house and warn him, turn to page 51.

"You do it, Jessica," you say.

"Okay. But stand next to me!"

You open the door. You are right in front of a desk. A tall blonde woman is standing behind it.

"Well, what do we have here?" she asks.

You forget all about Jessica and blurt out, "My dog's name is Homer, and he's lost."

Jessica gives your hand a squeeze. The woman stands up and says, "Right this way. We'll take care of it!"

Turn to page 20.

The woman shows you into an office and introduces you to Mike Watt, the radio deejay. He's the one who reads the news.

You explain the problem.

Mike Watt asks, "How about going on the air? You report on Homer. You've got a good voice."

It's scary, you think. Being on the air will be scary!

Turn to page 22.

Mike Watt takes you into a small sound-proof room and stands next to you. A red sign on the wall blinks "ON THE AIR." You clear your throat and speak into the microphone.

"My dog's name is Homer, and..."

Your message is going out to thousands of people! You feel proud of yourself.

Go on to the next page.

In just a few seconds you're done. You can't believe it was so easy!

Mike Watt says, "Great job. You really do have a perfect radio voice. Hey! How about doing a kids' radio program for us?"

If you tell him that you don't have time to talk about that right now because you're looking for Homer, turn to page 26.

If you say, "Yes, let's start right away," turn to page 30.

"Okay, okay, I'll do the talking. But what do I say?" you ask Jessica.

"Just act natural. Just talk to the people the way you talk to me. They don't bite. They don't even bark!" she says, laughing.

"Very funny, Jessica," you answer.

Go on to the next page.

Things go easily, and the radio station helps out. What a relief! The message about Homer will be broadcast at noon.

You decide not to wait at the station. Instead you'll keep looking for Homer. You can call the radio station later for messages.

If you go to look for Homer at the playground, turn to page 32.

If you check with the police to see if any dogs have been found, turn to page 57.

You promise Mike Watt that you'll be back after you find Homer. He says, "Don't let us down, now. You've got a future in radio!"

It's exciting when you imagine having your own kids' program. On the way home that's all you can think of.

Go on to the next page.

"What about Homer, big shot?" asks Jessica. That wakes you up from your daydream. She's right. Homer really is the most important thing. He comes first!

Turn to the next page.

Out of habit, you put your hand down to pat Homer. He gives you a juicy lick on the fingers.

"Stop that, Homer! Come on, stop it!" you say.

Then suddenly you realize what's happening.

"Homer! Homer! Where in the world did you come from?"

Homer just looks up and nudges you with his nose. If he could talk, he would probably say, "Aw, come on. You worry too much."

The End

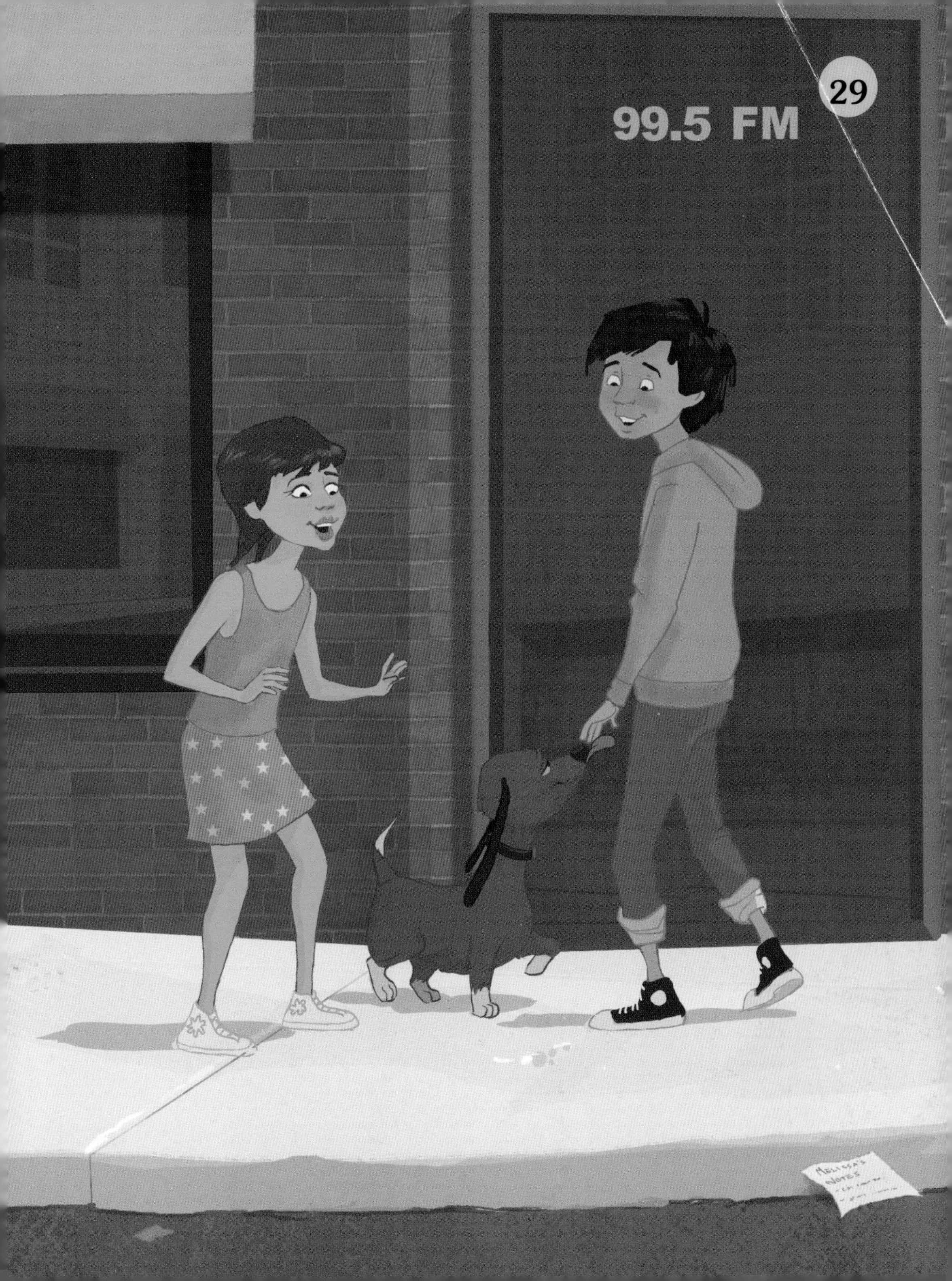
99.5 FM
MELISSA'S NOTES

Years later, when your children ask you how you became one of the world's most famous radio announcers, you tell them the story of the time Homer disappeared.

"But what happened to Homer?" they ask.

Go on to next page.

"Oh, he showed up. He wasn't lost after all. That's why my program was called 'Homer's Show.' It was my big break-through!"

The End

You and Jessica run toward the playground.

"Homer loves the playground," Jessica says.

"I only hope he's there!" you say.

But when you arrive at the playground, there is no Homer. As a matter of fact, there's only one person there—a little kid sitting in the sandbox.

"Boy, is he dirty!" says Jessica.

"Yeah. Wait until his mother sees him," you answer.

"Hey, have you seen a big brown-and-black dog around here?" you ask the boy.

He pours a pail of sand over his head.

Turn to page 34.

"Yup!" he answers. He keeps digging in the sand.

"Well, where is he?" you ask.

"I don't know," the boy says. Suddenly he gets up and runs away.

If you follow him, turn to page 40.

If you let him go and search the playground for Homer, turn to page 47.

"Okay, Homer, let Schooner know who's boss!" you say in your loudest voice.

Homer lets go with a huge bark, followed by an even bigger growl.

You stand your ground. "We mean business, Schooner. Leave us alone!" you say.

Turn to page 37.

Schooner adjusts his hat and looks at you.
"I'll let you go this time," he says. "But don't come back!"

You, Homer, and Jessica run out of the woods as fast as you can. You're safe!

The End

"Let's get out of here. Come on! Keep going!" you shout.

Schooner and his two friends are right behind you, yelling and screaming. Suddenly Homer stops short, turns around, and bares his teeth. He gives a low, fierce growl. You and Jessica stop to watch.

Go on to the next page.

Schooner raises his hand.

The fur on Homer's back rises in a ridge of black and brown bristles. He stands still, growling and barking.

Turn to page 44.

"Come on, Jessica. I'll bet he knows where Homer is. Follow me!" And you run off after the little boy.

He's fast, but finally you grab him by his dirty shirt.

"Got you!" you say.

"Let me go! Help! Let me go!" he screams. Just at that moment a woman in a floppy hat rushes up.

"Let Henry go at once!" she orders.

Turn to page 42.

"Yes, ma'am." You gulp and let go of
Henry. Jessica tries to hide behind you.

"We're just trying to find our dog Homer,"
you say.

"Well, this is a *boy*, not a dog." The woman
takes Henry by the ear and marches him off.

Go on to the next page.

"What now?" Jessica asks.

"Let's keep on looking," you reply. "We'll find him!"

The End

To continue looking for Homer, head to the police station by turning to page 57.

Schooner backs away slowly.

"I was only kidding. Honest, dog, I wasn't going to hurt these kids! Only kidding. Nice pooch, nice poochy," Schooner says.

Then Homer gives one giant bark. Schooner and his two friends take off like three rockets back toward the old fort.

"Nice work, Homer. You saved the day!" you say, giving Homer a big hug.

The End

You and Jessica slip away from your hiding place and run as fast as you can toward home.

"What about Homer?" Jessica yells.

"I don't know," you say. "Let's hurry. We'll have to find Homer later!"

Just then Homer dashes out of the woods and runs—thump!—right into you.

"Hey, Homer! Where did you come from?" you ask.

Homer gives several low barks and some worried growls.

"What is it, Homer? What is it, boy?"

Turn to page 54.

"That kid doesn't know what he's talking about. Come on, let's look down by the duck pond," you say to Jessica.

Moments later you are at the edge of a large pond. No Homer!

Turn to the next page.

Just then another little kid—a girl no more than three or four years old—slips into the pond. Her mother isn't watching!

You jump into the pond.

Turn to the next page.

"You're very brave," the little girl's mother says to you. "You saved my daughter's life. Why, without you—I don't even want to think what could have happened!"

She offers to take you home, but you and Jessica say no. "We have to find our dog Homer. He's lost," you say.

Boy, what a day! You hope it'll end soon—with Homer found.

The End

"Schooner and his gang are going to Old Pete's right now. We've got to warn Pete," you say. "I don't think we can make it home and back here with help in time."

Into the woods you go, following a narrow path. It doesn't take long to get to Old Pete's cabin.

Turn to the next page.

But no one's there.
No Homer, no Pete, no nothing!

If you decide to go into the cabin
and wait, hoping Pete will come
back, turn to page 61.

If you head back into the woods,
turn to page 72.

"Maybe he wants us to go with him. Probably to help Pete," you say.

"How could he know those bullies are going to rob Pete?" Jessica asks.

"Dogs have ways of knowing things," you answer.

Go on to the next page.

You follow Homer on the trail to Old Pete's cabin. You get there just in time! Schooner's gang is sneaking up on the cabin. Homer leaps forward, barking a warning.

Turn to page 69.

The police station sounds scary to you. What if Homer's been hit by a car? But you screw up your courage, and you and Jessica go into the station.

The policeman at the desk looks down at you and smiles. "Well, you didn't rob a bank, did you?" he says.

You explain about Homer. The policeman says, "I'll check it out right away."

Turn to the next page.

The policeman reads the reports on his desk carefully.

Then he calls the patrol car to ask if any dogs have been hit.

You all hear the patrol car answer over the two-way radio: "No dogs hit by any cars that we know of. No cats either."

Turn to the next page.

"Whew! Wow, I was really worried that Homer had been hit. Thanks, Officer. We'll keep on looking," you say.

"Jessica, we haven't even checked the dog pound yet," you say.

"You're right! Pretty dumb, huh? Let's go," she answers.

Turn to page 67.

The cabin is full of Pete's science experiments. You think you hear something upstairs. Is it Pete, or the bullies?

"Jessica, grab one of those pots and a wooden spoon. Beat on it when I tell you to. We'll scare Schooner and his gang away!"

Turn to page 63.

The noise upstairs gets louder. Just then, you see Schooner and his gang approaching from the clearing.

Turn to the next page.

Suddenly, there is an explosion from upstairs.

"Eureka!" yells Old Pete, and he and Homer come running down from the attic. Homer is barking excitedly. "We've done it!"

Between the explosion and Jessica banging the pots and pans, Schooner and his friends look very scared and run away.

Pete just laughs. "What a day," he says. "I haven't had so much excitement since the Fourth of July party—fourteen years ago!"

The End

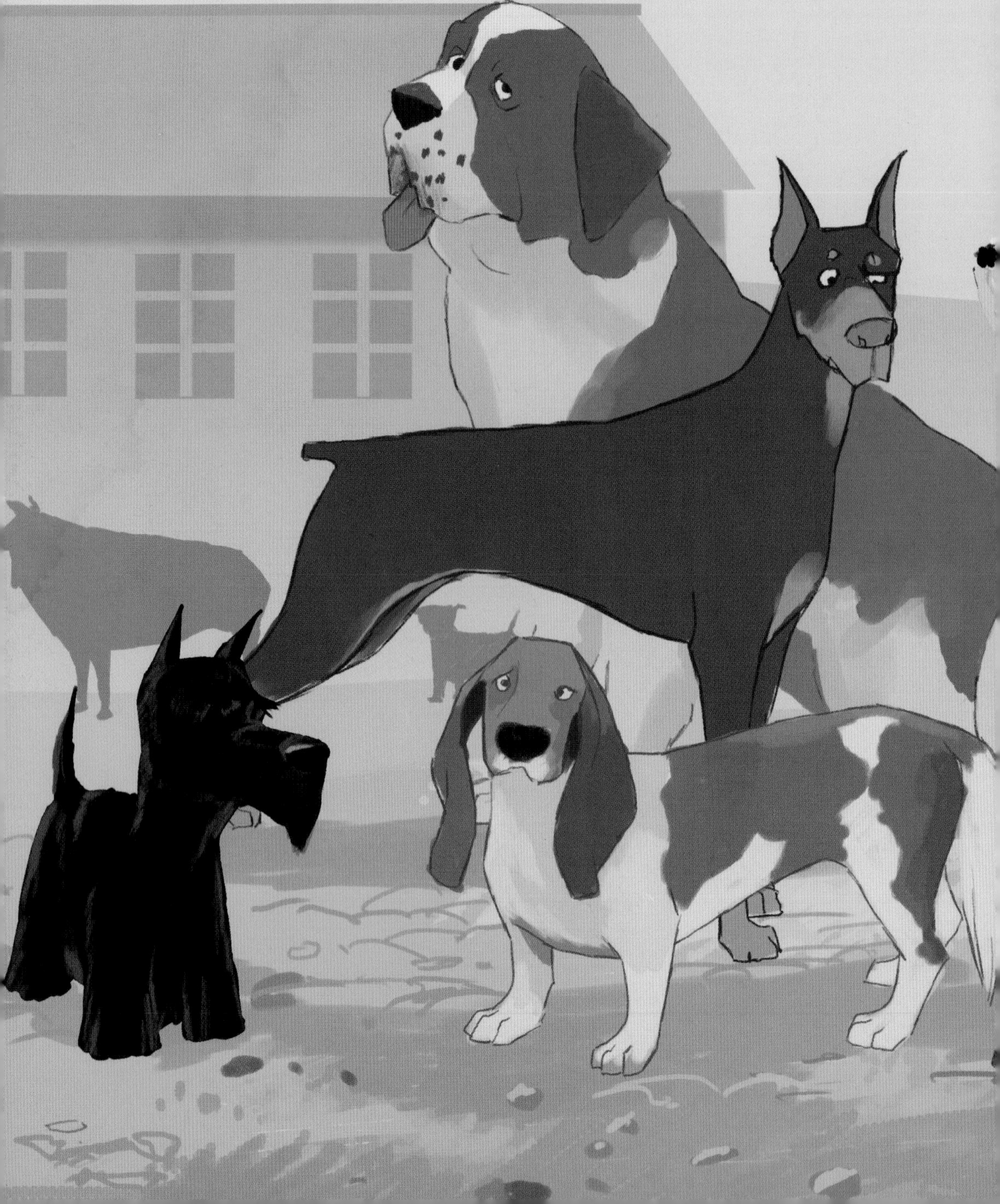

An hour later you peer through a fence at a pack of dogs in the pound.

Turn to the next page.

"Homer! Hey, Homer! It's us!" you shout.

Homer leaps at the fence—his tail wagging, tongue licking.

"Okay, Homer, you'll have to leave your new friends," you say. "Let's go home!"

The End

"Let's get out of here!" Schooner yells. He and the other two boys run off into the woods. Pete comes out of his cabin. "What's all this racket?" he says.

Turn to the next page.

"Schooner and his gang were after your money!" you say.

Pete gives a little laugh. "Well, there is no money," he says. "And what's more, I'm tired of Schooner. This time he's gone too far. I'm going to talk with Schooner's parents tonight!"

The End

Just then you hear a noise. It is a low, eerie sound, sort of like a loon and sort of like…"It sounds like Homer when he's sick," you shout to Jessica. "It must be Homer!"

The low moaning sound gets louder.

"Homer! Homer!" you shout.

But there is no answer.

You peer underneath the house. It isn't Homer! It's a little gray-and-black dog.

Turn to page 74.

"Nice dog. We're friendly," you say, reaching down to show the little dog your hand. Jessica backs away so the dog won't be scared.

Just at that moment, Homer appears, wagging all over. The dog under the house slowly crawls out. Then you notice its leg. It's hurt!

Homer nudges the little dog with his nose and whines. Now you understand. Homer has been trying to help!

Go on to the next page.

"Good Homer!" you say. "Jessica, you take this dog back home. Mom will know what to do about its leg. Homer and I will stay here and scare off Schooner's gang. Right, Homer?"

He gives a sound that's half-yowl, half-bark. You know he means, "You're right, boss!"

The End

ABOUT THE AUTHOR

R. A. Montgomery attended Hopkins Grammar School, Williston-Northhampton School and Williams College where he graduated in 1958. He pursued graduate studies in Religion and Economics at Yale and NYU. Montgomery was an adventurer all his life, climbing mountains in the Himalaya, skiing throughout Europe and scuba-diving wherever he could. His interests included education, macro-economics, geo-politics, mythology, history, mystery novels and music. He wrote his first interactive book, *Journey Under the Sea*, in 1976 and published it under the series name *The Adventures of You*. A few years later Bantam Books bought this book and gave Montgomery a contract for five more, to inaugurate their new children's publishing division. Bantam renamed the series *Choose Your Own Adventure* and a publishing phenomenon was born. The series has sold more than 260 million copies in over 40 languages. He was married to the writer Shannon Gilligan. Montgomery died in November 2014, only two months after his last book was published.

ABOUT THE ILLUSTRATOR

Illustrator Keith Newton began his art career in the theater as a set painter. Having talent and a strong desire to paint portraits, he moved to New York and studied fine art at the Art Students League. Keith has won numerous awards in art such as The Grumbacher Gold Medallion and Salmagundi Award for Pastel. He soon began illustrating and was hired by Walt Disney Feature Animation where he worked on such films as *Pocahontas* and *Mulan* as a background artist. Keith also designed color models for sculptures at Disney's Animal Kingdom and has animated commercials for Euro Disney. Today, Keith Newton freelances from his home and teaches entertainment illustration at the College for Creative Studies in Detroit. He is married and has two daughters.

For games, activities, and other fun stuff, or to write to Chooseco, visit us online at CYOA.com